ÁGUA

The Mysterious Portuguese Water Dog

Written by Reneé Kelahan

Illustrated by Penny Hauffe

For Alyssa,
Enjoy getting to
know Agua!!

Warmest Wishes,

Renee Kelahan

iUniverse, Inc.
New York   Bloomington

Água, the Mysterious Portuguese Water Dog

iUniverse books may be ordered through booksellers or by contacting:

iUniverse
1663 Liberty Drive
Bloomington, IN 47403
www.iuniverse.com
1-800-Authors (1-800-288-4677)

ISBN: 978-1-4401-5442-3 (pbk)
ISBN: 978-1-4401-5443-0 (cloth)
ISBN: 978-1-4401-5444-7 (ebk)

Library of Congress Control Number: 2009931616

Printed in the United States of America

iUniverse rev. date: 10/6/2009

Dedication

To my husband, Matt, and my children,
Casey, and Cameron, for supporting and
encouraging me in my writing efforts.

And to Nalu, our first dog, the smartest, funniest, most
loyal Portie ever and my inspiration for this book.

~ RK

Author's Note

Portuguese Water Dogs (Porties) are loyal companions and are strong, brave, protective, and very intelligent. They are part of the American Kennel Club Working Dog Group and need to be kept busy with jobs and plenty of exercise. They like being with their people and do not like being left alone for long.

Not everyone is meant to be a Portie owner and not just because of the high cost of purchasing one. Before acquiring one, please research the breed and its characteristics and decide if it is really the right type of dog for you. Both you and the dog will be much happier if you are a good fit for each other. A good resource for information is the Portuguese Water Dog Club of America at www.pwdca.org.

Portugal

Porto

Lisbon

Atlantic Ocean

ALGARVE

Salema

Cape St. Vincent   Lagos   Gulf of
Cadiz

Portugal in Relation to the Rest of Europe

Iceland

Norway

Finland

Sweden

Estonia

Russia

Denmark

Latvia

Lithuania

Ireland

United Kingdom

Netherlands

Belarus

Belgium

Germany

Poland

Czech Rep

Slovakia

Ukraine

Switzerland

Austria

Hungary

Slovenia

Croatia

Romania

Portugal

France

Italy

Bosnia

Serbia

Bulgaria

Macedonia

Portugal

Spain

Albania

Greece

Turkey

Atlantic Ocean

Chapter 1

Silent tears slid down twelve-year-old Natalia's face as she looked out the window. Her father and younger brother were walking home from the waterfront; and even from this distance, she could see the dejected slump of their shoulders. Through the falling dusk, she could see that, once again, they had little to show for a full day of fishing.

Natalia and her brother, Tomas, were learning at a young age that the sea could be cruel. Months had passed since anyone in the Portuguese fishing village of Salema could claim a successful catch for even a single day. The little town was withering away, like *uvas velhas* (old grapes) on the vine. Slowly, one by one, people were packing up and leaving for the mountains to find a new, more stable life as sheep herders. But Natalia's family could not leave because of Mama. Mama ...

Natalia's head drooped, and her shiny black curls spilled forward like a curtain around her sun-kissed face. She dreaded telling Mama that yet another day had come and gone with Papa and Tomas returning home empty handed. Mama was so brave and strong, more than any of the rest of them, even though the mystery illness was slowly wearing her away. Natalia had heard the neighbor women murmuring something about *escorbuto* (scurvy) and clucking their tongues about how it was a shame that such a fine young woman as Olivia had fallen so ill. Natalia also heard the women saying that just a bit of fresh fruit could help her Mama get better. But they could not grow it so far south along the coast, and it had been months since any of the village families had fish to sell or trade in the nearby city of Lagos. Every day Mama's inner light seemed to dim just a little more, and Natalia was afraid it would soon flicker out, never to brighten their world again.

Slowly, she straightened and turned from the window, wiping her eyes with her apron as she went. She bravely put on a cheerful face and stepped into the small alcove just off the kitchen area where her mother quietly rested on a lumpy old mattress. Mama's bright, keen eyes found hers. She smiled tiredly but determinedly and slowly lifted a hand toward her daughter. "The men are on their way back, are they?" she asked.

"Yes," Natalia replied, taking her mother's hand. "It seems that *o mar* (the sea) has once again not given father and Tomas the big catch we have been praying for."

"Ah, so that is why your eyes are so sad, my daughter. Have faith. Remember, the Lord moves in mysterious ways."

Chapter 2

Tired from a long day of cooking, caring for her mother, and repairing fishing nets, Natalia quietly went about preparing dinner that night. In the not too distant past she would have been happily humming one of the local *chulas* (folk songs), but tonight there was not much happiness in the little fishing hut. Dinner was a simple meal of *feijoada* (bean stew) and flat bread that Natalia had been given by a neighbor earlier in the day. Everyone was quiet, as there seemed little to say. Mama was not able to come to the table that night and ate few of the spoonfuls that Natalia tried to feed her. Shadows filled the little hut, cast from a single oil lamp set in the middle of the table, a lamp that would soon be empty because they had no oil to refill it.

After dinner, Mama dozed off, her rosary still clasped in her hands. Natalia cleaned up the cooking area, while Papa read aloud from the Bible. She closed her eyes and listened. And she prayed with all her heart that God was watching over them, that Mama would get better, and that somehow a miracle would come along to keep the little fishing village alive.

Father and Tomas soon turned in for the night, sharing a small pallet and ragged blanket in a corner of the little hut. Natalia dimmed the oil lamp and carried it to her mother's room where she slept beside her every night on a pallet on the floor. She walked to the window to close the lace curtains. As she did so, she noticed a wispy fog creeping in low upon the sea. A light shiver ran through her, for as a little girl she had heard reverently whispered stories (stories she was not meant to hear) about mysterious occurrences that happened whenever this particular fog drifted in. *"Névoa do milagre"*

5

("miracle fog") the villagers called it. At the same time, off in the distance, Natalia thought she heard the echoing sound of a dog barking. Yet she knew that no dogs remained in or even around the little village.

Giving a sigh and turning from the window, Natalia changed into a flannel nightgown and climbed under the rough woolen blanket. But, tired as she was, she could not sleep. Her thoughts kept returning to the fog and what it might mean. She lay awake for what seemed like hours, when she thought she heard an odd scratching sound coming from somewhere close by. Then it stopped, only to start again moments later. Natalia slowly pulled back the blanket and quietly stood up. She tiptoed silently across the dark room and peered into the main area. The sound seemed to be coming from the door and grew louder as the moments went by.

Natalia was undecided. Should she wake her father and brother? Or should she investigate the noise herself? The memory of the fog and her own curiosity got the better of her, and she lit the lantern and quietly moved toward the door.

Chapter 3

Natalia opened the door a crack and peeked out. At first she saw nothing, but then a small noise made her look down. There, sitting on the doorstep, was a dog. Its hair was black and white and curly, and Natalia could see that it was soaking wet and shivering. It gazed up at her with peaceful, trusting brown eyes as if to say, "Will you take me in and care for me?" Unsure of what to do, Natalia opened the door wider. As she did so, the dog stood up and padded into the little hut. Upon closer inspection, she decided he was male and was bigger than she had first thought, a solid animal with a large head and long ears, broad shoulders, narrow hips, larger-than-expected feet, and with a tail that, oddly enough, curled up and over his back. Remarkably, the tail had a fluffy plume of white fur on its tip that waved like a flag in the air. His hair from waist to tail was shorter than the hair on his upper body and head. In fact, he had a lion-like look with a stance that could only be described as *régio* (regal).

Natalia had never seen anything quite like him. She watched as he lifted his nose in the air, sniffing as if perhaps he could sense something about the occupants of the home. Satisfied, he turned and walked back toward Natalia, who was still holding the door. He sat down in front of her, wagging his impossibly curly tail back and forth and staring at her with expectant eyes. "Hello, boy," she offered. "Where did you come from?" She held out her hand, and he licked it softly. As if he understood her question, he looked at the door and gave a low woof. Natalia sensed that he was asking her to close the door, so she did. The dog moved closer to her, leaning against her legs and pressing her back into the room

Once again, Natalia noticed how wet he was, so she went in search of a rag to dry him with. He followed closely behind her, as if he could not bear to be separated from her. Natalia knelt in front of him and, as she dried him, she talked softly to him. "Who is your owner, and what is your name, I wonder?" He stared at her patiently. "No matter. For now I shall call you *Água*, as you have obviously come to me from out of the water. In the morning I shall see if I can somehow find your owner." She then turned and walked back to her pallet, settling down once again to sleep. Only this time, she had a companion who lay close by her side as she drifted off to sleep. And as Água laid his head down on his large paws, unbeknown to Natalia, the miracle fog slowly drifted back out to sea.

Chapter 4

The morning dawned clear and bright. Natalia awakened at the first crack of light that shone through the window. She lay with her eyes closed, thinking of the dream she had the night before of the majestic dog who had come to her in the night. "What an odd dream," she thought, as she stretched, one arm extending out to her side. She started as she touched the softest fur she had ever felt. Sitting up abruptly, she turned to see the creature she remembered from her dream lying at her side, sleeping deeply as if he had been on a long journey and was now able to rest.

Natalia's hand flew to her mouth. It had not been a dream after all! Água really did exist! She turned on her side and looked more closely at him. In the dim light of the lantern last night, she had not noticed that he had a white streak down the center of his curly head and totally white front legs. And he had a fringe of bang that hung over his now closed eyes. As she watched him, he opened his eyes, which were a deeper, darker brown than she remembered. As he quickly blinked his right eye closed and then open again, she was sure that he had purposely winked at her! Shaking her head at her fanciful thoughts, Natalia softly said, "Good morning, Água. Did you sleep well?" In answer, he rolled on to his back and stretched, arching his back and presenting his stomach to her for attention. She laughed quietly and said, "All right, boy, I will pet your stomach," and she reached out and rubbed him back and forth, again marveling at the softness of what most people would think was fur but which felt more like human hair.

"Well, boy," Natalia again said softly so that she would not wake Mama. "We cannot lie here all morning. I must get up and prepare breakfast for Papa and Tomas before they go off to fish for the day. Here we go." She stood up and quietly rolled up her pallet then reached for her seven-flannel skirt, cotton top, and the apron that her mother had lovingly embroidered for her as a gift on her tenth birthday. Natalia never could look at her apron without smiling in wonderment at the time and love her Mama had put into it. She quickly changed out of her nightgown and into her clothes, smoothing the skirt and apron as she stood looking at Mama, who was still sleeping fitfully. She said a quick prayer and turned to walk out into the next room.

Chapter 5

Papa and Tomas had already awakened, and Natalia could see through the window that they were examining the nets she had mended yesterday. They had brought several more back from the boat with them last night, so she knew she would be busy again today. She also had several nets from neighbor fishermen to repair in trade for small amounts of flour, sugar, and beans.

Água had followed her out into the small room, peering around him as if deciding where to settle. He walked over toward the door and laid down in a most unusual position, his front paws extended straight out, as were his back legs. He looked utterly relaxed. Natalia laughed as she looked at him. "Making yourself right at home, I see! Well, do not get too comfortable there, boy, for I must make breakfast and then introduce you to father and Tomas." Água wagged his tail and cocked his head to one side, and, once again, she was sure he winked at her!

As Água looked on contentedly, Natalia cut pieces from a sweetbread loaf that her family had been given the day before. Breakfast was a very simple affair, even in better times. The men were always eager to get out on the ocean early in the morning for the best catches of the day. Before calling her father and brother in, Natalia looked in on her mother. She was still asleep, but she did not seem comfortable, as her head kept turning from side to side. Natalia tucked the blanket in a little more closely around her, said a short prayer for her mother's renewed health, and turned to go toward the door.

As Natalia drew near him, Água stood up and stretched mightily with his front feet sliding forward as far as they would go while his back legs stayed in place. This created a comical image, for his bottom stuck up in the air, and his plumed tail flew like a flag. Natalia laughed and ran her hand down his soft, fluffy back. Água then stood up straight and nuzzled her hand for more attention. Again she laughed, a merry sound that had not been heard for quite a while in the little hut. "Yes, yes, Água! We will go meet Papa and Tomas now. I am still not quite sure how I am going to explain you to them."

Natalia opened the door and took a step as if to go out, expecting Água to follow her. Instead, he suddenly came to an alert position and then took off running. She thought he was running toward Papa and Tomas, but as she watched him, he ran toward the dock down on the ocean inlet. Água's ears and hair were blowing back, he ran so fast. And he began barking furiously as he went.

Chapter 6

Father and Tomas stood and watched Água bolt out of the fishing hut and tear past them, their mouths falling open in surprise. "*Que era aquele?*" (What was that?) her father asked. "*Um cão de água, Papa.* (A water dog, Papa). He came to the door last night while you and Tomas were asleep. He was all wet and looked so lost and alone that I brought him in, dried him off, and let him sleep next to me last night. I intend to ask around the village this morning to find out if anyone knows anything about him, but I do not know what he is doing now."

Natalia, her Papa, and Tomas all watched in amazement as Água sprinted down the short dock and made a running leap off the end. With a loud SPLASH! they heard him enter the water. The three of them began to run down to the dock to see what he was doing. As they approached, they saw no sign of him! Where had he gone? Suddenly his head broke through the surface of the water, and in his mouth was a fish! And not just any fish, but a large sea bass that looked as if it would make fish stew for ten people! "*Elogie o Senhor!*" (Praise the Lord) her father said, dropping to his knees in the sand. Água's catch was the first fish anyone had seen in two months in the little village.

Chapter 7

Água quickly swam to shore, the treasure in his mouth. He waded out of the surf and up onto the sand, where he gave a hard shake from the top of his head to the very tip of his tail. Sparkling drops flew everywhere.

He scanned the beach, quickly spotting Natalia and her family. He broke into a proud, prancing trot toward her as if to say, "Look at me! Look what I have!" He stopped directly in front of her, sat down immediately, and proudly held the fish, awaiting her praise. "Good boy, Água!" Natalia said, dropping down to give him a big hug.

As she continued to talk to him in a gentle, loving voice, Água turned his head slightly to look at her father and Tomas. Papa had stood up again, hugging Tomas to his side, tears of happiness rolling slowly down his face. Papa gently let go of Tomas and stepped up next to Água, extending his hand as he did so. Água promptly dropped the fish in Papa's hand, and a strong, loyal friendship was born.

Chapter 8

Natalia, Tomas, and her Papa started to dance around with
joy on the beach, Água jumping and yelping at their side.
Soon their neighbors came down see what the commotion
was all about. When they saw the fish Papa was holding,
they immediately understood and began to dance and sing as
well. But soon the men realized that the morning was quickly
passing, as was their chance to fill their nets with more fish.
They hurriedly ran to their boats, which they dragged up on
the beach each night, and pushed them out into the small
inlet. Then they swiftly rowed out into the sea and headed
for deeper waters.

As soon as Papa and Tomas had run to their boat and
begun pushing it toward the water, Água had jumped in the
aft and stood facing the sea. He began to bark joyfully, his
tail sweeping back and forth. As soon as their boat entered
the water, he quieted suddenly. As Papa brought the boat
about, Água moved to stand in the prow. He seemed to be
looking out even beyond the horizon, seeing something that
no human could see. At the same time, Natalia turned and
headed back up the beach to tell Mama the wonderful news.
Little did she know that soon they would all know the mysti-
cal power of Água.

Chapter 9

The smell of saltwater, like none other on Earth, filled their nostrils as they rowed on. Tomas could see that all of the fishing boats from the village had fallen in behind Papa's boat, their owners praying that Água would lead them to even more bounty. Água continued to stare straight ahead for a quite a while. Then his head turned to the right, and he came to attention. Noticing this, Papa turned the little boat in the direction of Água's stare.

They continued on for a while. The only sound was that of the ocean's white caps slapping on the side of the little boat, the *Esperança* (Hope). Just as Tomas was beginning to wonder when they would get to the right fishing spot, Água began an excited dance, spinning in circles and yipping excitedly. "What is it, boy?" Tomas said. "Do you sense *peixes*?" (fish)

In answer, Água sprung up and over the side of the boat, landing again with a loud SPLASH! He began swimming in tight circles next to them and barking as if to say, "Right here! Right here!" All of the fishing boats spread out around him and begin expertly throwing their casting nets overboard. One by one, Água towed the nets to exactly where he wanted them. Then the weights on the nets allowed them to sink below the surface in search of their prize.

Chapter 10

When he was done placing the nets, Água swam back to the *Esperança*, where Tomas and Papa hauled him back up into the boat. "*Bom cao* (good dog)," Tomas said, as Água shook himself from head to tail. Tomas noticed that Papa was peering intently into the water, as if trying to will the fish into the net. Água stepped up close to Papa and looked down in the water, too. Then he reached down and grabbed in his teeth the line that attached the net to the boat. He tugged hard, sitting back on his haunches and pushing with both of his front feet against the side of the boat, growling low in his throat with the effort. Papa and Tomas quickly stepped in to help and could not believe the amount of weight they felt as they pulled on the net.

Slowly but steadily, the man, the boy, and the dog hauled the net closer and closer until it was resting against the side of the boat. With one last mighty pull, the three of them lifted the heavy net on board. There, before their eyes, was the biggest catch of sea bass, mackerel, and sardines they had ever seen! Papa and Tomas stood speechless while Água stood there wagging his tail back and forth and looking at them as if to say, "Look what we did!"

All around them the other little fishing boats were pulling in equally large hauls. Great shouts of joy rang out over the water as the fishermen gave thanks for their change in fortune. "Let us go share our good news, Água," Papa said, and he began to row for home.

Chapter 11

Long before the boats were fully in view, Natalia heard the sound of jubilant singing rolling over the waves toward shore. In the background she heard the excited barking of a dog, which meant it could only be the men coming home already with Água at their side. She dropped the net she had been mending and ran to the little hut. Throwing the door wide, Natalia ran in calling to her mother. "Mama! Mama! I hear the men coming, and they are singing a joyous song! They must have had great luck today! Surely our fortunes are changing!"

Mama smiled weakly. "I am overjoyed, *minha filha* (my daughter). We will praise God tonight, for our prayers have been answered." Looking at her Mama, Natalia prayed with all her heart that her other prayer would soon be answered, that Mama would be healthy again. Leaning down, she gently kissed her Mama's cheek and told her that she was going down to the dock to meet the boats as they came in. Mama had already drifted off to sleep again, so Natalia quietly left the hut and ran down to the beach.

Chapter 12

The men were pulling the boats ashore when Natalia arrived at the dock. Seeing her, Tomas waved and called out, "Irma! Irma! (Sister! Sister!) We have brought back more fish in our nets than I have ever seen in my life! Every one of our boats has nets full of sea bass, mackerel, and sardines!"

"Yes, Natalia," called Papa. "We must celebrate tonight with our neighbors. Hurry, child, and get the other women to come and help clean the fish." Natalia did as her father asked and turned and ran to the cluster of huts further along the beach.

"*Amigas! Vizinhos!* (Friends! Neighbors!) Come quickly to the dock! The men are back, and they have a magnificent catch!"

All of the women and small children ran to the beach and hugged and kissed their husbands, fathers, sons, and brothers. Then they all went to each boat one by one and together lifted out bursting nets, more than any family could handle alone. At the first touch of land, Água had jumped out of the boat and run to Natalia. Tears of happiness streamed down Natalia's face as she threw her arms around Água's neck and buried her face in his soft fur saying, "You are truly a blessing, Água!" He gently pulled away until he could lick her face, then he pushed on her with his nose, as if to say there was work to be done. Natalia and Água joined the others, and when a fish fell out of a net here or there, Água was there to gently scoop it up and return it.

As the work of cleaning the fish began, the women talked excitedly about the day's events and the wonder dog who had come into their midst. Natalia quickly explained how Água had come to be in their village and how she was planning on trying to locate his owner. The other women looked at her in dismay, wondering silently if their good fortune would hold without this miracle dog.

Chapter 13

Several days passed, and the men of the village continued their successful fishing, Água always at their side. Natalia had been unsuccessful at finding his owner, so he continued to live with her and her family. Then, one day, as she was working cleaning fish, Natalia suddenly heard Tomas urgently calling to her. "Natalia! *Irmã!* Mama is calling for you. Come quickly!" Natalia dropped her knife and spun away to run up the beach to the hut, Água close on her heels.

She hurried through the open door and quickly moved to Mama's bedside. Her voice barely above a whisper, Mama said, "Natalia, meu *cara* (my dear), I can feel that time is getting short. I wish to tell you how much you mean to me and how I will always watch over you and Papa and Tomas after I am gone."

"No, no, Mama!" Natalia cried as she dropped down beside the bed sobbing, taking Mama's hand in hers and holding it to her cheek. Água immediately sensed how ill Mama was and laid his head on the bed next to her and whined softly.

"Oh, Mama," Natalia cried, "if only we could get some fresh fruit from the city you would get better! I know you would! How can we sit and do nothing? If only we had time to catch more fish to sell, but we do not. How can we get enough money to buy the fruit for you?"

Just then Água sat up and went on alert, a low rumbling growl sounding in his throat. "What is it, boy?" Natalia asked, her hand going to his neck. Água moved slowly toward the door, step by step, growling louder now. Then, suddenly, a knock came on the door.

Chapter 14

Natalia went to open the door, but Água quickly stepped in front of her and leaned back against her legs to stop her. Through the closed door, she could now hear Papa talking to another man, one whose voice she did not recognize. "So, Paulo, I hear that you have found yourself a miracle dog and that he has brought you good luck. I could use such a dog in my fishing fleet in Lagos. I have come to make you a handsome offer for him."

"The dog is not for sale, Dom Filipe. He is not ours to sell. He has adopted us, and we are grateful for the time he is with us. He has restored the good fortune of Salema, *agradeça ao Deus* (thank God)."

"But, Paulo, I hear that your wife, Olivia, has been quite ill and that money would allow you to go to the city to buy what she needs to cure her condition. Is that not so?"

"Yes, it is so, but this is not my decision to make. The dog is here of his own free will and has attached himself to my daughter. He is an animal of great spirit and pride, I can see. He makes his own choices."

At that, Água stopped pressing on Natalia and moved toward to door, pawing at it as if asking to go outside. Natalia stepped to the door and swung it open. Água stood for a moment staring at the man, Dom Filipe, pinning him with his eyes. Hearing the door open, Dom Filipe looked down, locking eyes with Água. After a moment he said, "So, this is the dog I have been hearing so much about, eh?" Água continued to stare at him, distrust evident in his slightly crouched stance.

Natalia stepped through the door and was introduced by Papa to Dom Filipe, one of the wealthiest men in the Algarve.

He was a portly man with beady dark eyes and a complexion that showed that he had never worked long hours in the sun like a true fisherman. A sinister-looking scar ran from his left eyebrow down to his cheek. He smiled crookedly at her and said, "Well, young lady, I hear that you are the one to talk to about this amazing dog. What is it that you call him?"

" Água," Natalia replied briefly.

"And how do you come to own such a magnificent animal, may I ask?"

Natalia told Dom Filipe the short story of Água's arrival in the middle of the night and how he had adopted her family and the little village of Salema. "He does not truly belong to you then?" Dom Filipe asked. Before she could answer, Água turned and went to her side. He sat down by her as if to say, "I belong to Natalia and no other. I am hers to do with as she wishes."

Chapter 15

Dom Filipe took in the scene and nodded his head. "It seems that the beast has decided who owns him. Very well, I shall make you the offer that I just made your father. I am prepared to pay handsomely for him. You will then have money to go to Lagos immediately to get fruit and herbs for your mother to help cure her. Is this not what you want?"

Natalia placed her hand on Água's head. She felt the curly hair under her fingers as she slowly petted him. She looked down at him, and he looked up at her as if to say, "It's all right. I know that you need to help your Mama."

After a long moment, choking on the words, Natalia agreed to sell Água to Dom Filipe. "But only on one condition."

"And what might that be," Dom Filipe asked suspiciously.

Natalia replied, "I must be allowed to take Água with me on the trip to Lagos. I am the one who will have to travel there, as Papa and Tomas must continue to fish. I will need a protector along the way. As soon as we return, I will turn Água over to you." Again, she could barely say the words.

Feeling generous, Dom Filipe said, "Certainly, my dear. You may take the dog with you. But let us understand each other: immediately upon your return, he is mine."

Chapter 16

After a long night of tossing and turning, Natalia finally rose at first light. Again, her faithful Água had slept close by her side all night. Mama was still sleeping, so Natalia quickly dressed and rolled up her pallet. She knelt by her mama's bedside for moment in prayer and then said a soft goodbye.

She went in search of Papa and Tomas and saw that they were already outside preparing for a day of fishing. Last night, the three of them had sat and talked for a long time planning the journey she was about to take. They had decided that she would leave at first light and that she would carry four small fishing nets that she and Água could use to carry the fruit back to Salema. She and Tomas had laughed together about the memories they had of when they were young children learning to cast a net by using them. Who knew then what an important role those nets would play one day?

They agreed that she and Água would need to stay overnight one night in Lagos, taking sanctuary at the *Igreja de Santo Antonio* (Church of Saint Antonio). They also agreed that while Natalia was gone Mama would be taken care of during the day by one of her friends.

Natalia placed several pieces of bread and a hunk of cheese wrapped in wax into the large pocket on the inside of her apron. She also patted the corner of the pocket to reassure herself that the money was really there. Yes, there it was: the money from Dom Filipe. She had not made it up. Natalia sighed with relief.

While she was preparing, Água sat patiently, watching her every move. When she was ready to go outside, Natalia walked over to him and dropped down to the floor, eye to eye. "Agua," she said, "we are leaving on a very important journey. You are my eyes and ears, my *protetor bravo* (brave protector)." In answer, Água licked her face. Natalia laughed. "Good boy! Let us go find Papa and Tomas." And together they walked out the door.

Chapter 17

Natalia hugged Papa and Tomas tightly. Papa whispered a prayer for safe travel in her ear. Then she picked up the nets and said, "Adeus!" (goodbye), and she and Água headed for the trail that would take them to Lagos. "*Boa sorte!*" (good luck) and "*Boa viagem!*" (have a safe journey) all of the villagers called to them.

The day was beginning as most did in the Algarve region of southern Portugal, clear and sunny and promising to be quite warm. The sky was azure blue and cloudless. As they walked along briskly, Natalia talked to Água about the beauty all around them. "Oh, Água, we live in the most beautiful place in the world! God has truly blessed us!" Along the path, they saw wild jasmine glowing with tiny yellow blossoms, dog rose bushes with pale pink blooms peeping through, and sage leaf rockrose bursting with small white flowers. Smiling, Natalia vowed to make a bouquet for Mama on the way home.

The path was well worn by frequent travelers between Salema and Lagos, so Natalia and Água had no difficulty finding their way. Água often dashed ahead, barking excitedly. He was discovering a few of the many birds in the area like Bee-eaters, Hoopoe, and Spotless Starlings. Once he even flushed a Red Legged Partridge. Natalia had to laugh! She did not know who looked more startled, Água or the bird! Then he dove headlong into the underbrush searching for more.

"Água, come here, boy," she called. "We do not have time to play right now. Perhaps on the way back you will find more friends." She could see the flying flag of his tail heading back toward the path, and suddenly he burst through the brush.

She laughed out loud because he was covered in pollen and looked quite comical with pieces of plant stuck to his curly fur. His tongue was lolling from exertion, and he looked like he was smiling! "You are such a happy dog, Água!" Natalia said as she brushed him off with her hand.

They continued on for a while, stopping to rest under a large, shady Judas tree laden with magenta pink flowers. The sun was high in the sky, and Natalia's stomach was rumbling. "Time for a bite to eat, Água?" He gave a short "Woof!" in response, and Natalia reached into her apron pocket and pulled out the bread and cheese. She broke off a hunk of bread and offered it to Água, who gently took it from her hand. His muzzle was as soft as moss in the spring, Natalia thought. She then gave him a piece of cheese, which he gently but hungrily swallowed right down. "I know, boy, this is not much for us to eat. But soon we will be in Lagos buying fruit, and I promise you I will buy you a treat." Natalia quickly finished her share of the meal, and they were off again.

Chapter 18

They walked along in companionable silence for quite a while. Then once again Água ran ahead around a bend in the path. When Natalia got there, he was nowhere to be seen.

"Água!" she called. "Água!" A short distance off the path, she heard him bark in response. She made her way to him as he continued to give short barks to guide her. She came upon him sitting quite calmly next to a gurgling stream. His muzzle was all wet so she could see that he had been quite thirsty and was now inviting her to drink. "Oh, Água!" Natalia said. "I am thirsty, too. Thank you for finding us water to drink!" Papa had told her that the streams in the area were safe to drink from, but they had not seen one yet on their journey.

Natalia set the nets down on the ground and knelt down next to the stream. She leaned over and cupped her hands, filling them with water and drinking thirstily. As she focused on her task, she did not notice a slight movement just off her right side. Água did. He stiffened and suddenly sprang up and pounced on something on the ground. Natalia jumped up, startled by his sudden movement. There, under Água's paws, she saw a snake! It was bluish, with a white underbelly and looked quite threatening with its heavily hooded eyes.

Papa had warned her to watch out for the snakes that roamed the area. Água had pinned one of the more danger-ous ones, a Montpellier snake. Though Natalia knew that its venom would not kill her, it could have made her quite sick and unable to continue her trip. Água had saved her! He grabbed the snake in his teeth and gave his head a mighty shake, sending the snake hurtling off into the tall grass.

Sobbing with relief, Natalia dropped down next to Água and hugged him close. "You see," she said to him, "you are *meu protetor*! Thank you! Thank you!" After a moment, Natalia let him go and picked up the nets. She wiped her tears and said, "Let's go boy. We are almost to Lagos." And they set off again.

Chapter 19

Arriving in the city of Lagos just as the sun was setting, Natalia and Água stopped and looked around. The small city sat high on the cliffs along the *Oceano Atlântico*, commanding a spectacular view and serving as a center for trading. Natalia's Papa had told her that until 100 years ago in 1755, Lagos was the proudest city in all the Algarve; but a disastrous earthquake, followed by a gigantic wave, had destroyed much of Portugal, including the Algarve.

Shaking her head to bring herself back to the present, Natalia looked down at Água and said, "Well, boy, we need to find the *Igreja de Santo Antonio,* where Papa told us we can ask to spend the night. How do you think we should find it?" Just then, church bells started ringing, and Água began to dance in circles excitedly.

"Is that the one, Água? Shall we go see?"

Água dashed off ahead of Natalia, listening all the time to the ringing bell. She ran after him, and he often stopped for a moment to look back to make sure she was still there. Soon they came upon a magnificent site. There, set against the sunset, was the *Igreja de Santo Antonio,* framed on either side by towering Agave trees.

Chapter 20

"Oh, Água," Natalia whispered. "Have you ever seen anything so beautiful?" Água wagged his tail in agreement. Then he began walking toward the church, looking back expectantly for Natalia to follow. Together, they approached the large, wooden doors. Natalia hesitated for a moment in front of them, but Água confidently sat down and raised his paw to scratch on the door.

"Yes, Água," Natalia smilingly said. "You are much braver than I am!" She reached into her apron pocket and pulled out a small piece of lace cloth to cover her head as a sign of respect as Papa had told her to. Then she slowly reached up and opened one of the doors. On creaky hinges, it slowly swung open until Natalia and Água could see inside. Since dusk was falling, the interior was quite dim except for a number of burning candles.

Natalia stepped forward, dropped down on one knee, and made the sign of the cross from her forehead to her chest, then from left to right shoulder. "*Em nome do Pai, do Filho, e do Espírito Santo. Amen,*" Natalia said as her Papa had taught her last night. ("In the name of the Father, the Son, and the Holy Spirit. Amen.") He said this was the correct way for a Catholic to enter a church in order to give respect to God.

Água cocked his head and looked at her curiously, his tail making a swishing sound as it swept back and forth on the tile floor. Natalia petted him on the head and said, "I think that now we must look for *o padre*" (the priest). As she said this, a man stepped out from a side room into the candlelight.

"Good evening. I am Father Peres. How may I help you, *minha filha?*

"Good evening, *padre*. I am sorry for intruding. My name is Natalia, and I am from the little village of Salema. I am on a journey of great importance to my family. You see, my Mama is sick and needs to have fresh fruit and special herbs to get well. I have come here with my dog, Água, to buy fruit in the market tomorrow and return home. But we need a place to stay for the night. I promise that we will not be any trouble and will leave at first light."

The *padre* smiled. "Do not worry, *minha criança*" (my child). You are welcome to *santuário* (sanctuary) here in the house of God. You and your dog will be safe here. Please make yourselves comfortable here on one of the pews. I will get you a blanket to keep you warm. And I am sure that your friend, Água, will stay close as well."

Hearing his name spoken so kindly, Água, walked over to the priest and licked his hand. "*Abençoe-o, cão pequeno.* (Bless you, little dog.) And bless you, too, Natalia," he said as he stepped forward and laid his hand on her head. Then he turned and went out to find the blanket he had promised.

Chapter 21

Natalia had not thought she would sleep a wink, but as soon as she lay down on the pew and snuggled under the blanket, Água close by her side, she fell fast asleep. She awoke to Água licking her face. "Oh, Água," she laughed. "I knew I could count on you to get us going this morning." As she sat up and stretched, she looked around the church and stared in amazement. She had not been able to see well in the falling darkness, but now the bright sunlight of morning streamed in through the windows.

All around her were beautiful, gilded, intricately carved walls; exquisite blue and white *azulejos* (tiles); and huge paintings of religious scenes and people. Papa had told her that there was never a more beautiful church in the world, and now she could see why. Just then, the *padre* re-appeared carrying two sweet rolls, cheese, a jug, and a bowl.

"Good morning! I thought you might be awake by now," he said.

"Yes, thank you, Father. And good morning to you, too. Água and I were just admiring your beautiful church."

"God has been good to us, Natalia. *Igreja de Santo Antonio* is one of the few churches to have survived the great earthquake. Lagos has been rebuilding for one hundred years. But much was lost, and there is still a great deal to be done. The people have given greatly of themselves for the city and its churches."

"Yes, my Papa told me of the earthquake and great wave many years ago. He says that my village was almost destroyed, too."

"Well, my child, those days are behind us; and we pray for good days ahead. And now, you and Água should eat breakfast. Afterward I will escort you to the market and introduce you to our merchants. Do you have money to buy what you need?"

"Yes, Father, I have money," Natalia said quietly, a sad little droop to her mouth, her hand reaching out to stroke Água. He seemed to understand because he nuzzled her in response. She fed him first and then ate herself. She poured water from the jug into his bowl and then had some herself. The priest could see that she loved her dog very much and that she was deeply troubled by something, but he did not ask her any more questions. Soon they were finished and left for the market.

Chapter 22

As they stepped out into the bright morning sunshine and walked along briskly, Father Peres told Natalia more about the history of Lagos. As he began to describe the other churches in the city, Natalia looked down at Água, only to discover that he was not with them. Stopping, she turned to look back toward the *Igreja de Santo Antonio*. About half way back toward the church, she saw Água busily digging a hole under a tree. She called him, "Água! Here, boy!" But he did not slow down for a moment. Natalia and Father Peres looked at each other curiously, shrugged their shoulders, and walked back to see what Água was up to.

By the time they got to him, he had already dug out a good size pile of dirt and was scratching at something in the bottom of the hole. Father Peres and Natalia leaned down for a closer look and caught a glimpse of something shiny and metal. Natalia spoke softly to Água, and he stopped digging and stepped back toward her. Father Peres reached down into the hole and carefully lifted out a gold chalice. *"Pai sagrado!"* (sacred Father) he whispered. Reverently he held the cup in his hands and gently brushed off the dirt.

"What is it, Father?" Natalia asked.

"In the time of the earthquake and flood much was lost," he answered. "When the churches were destroyed, many sacred items became buried or washed away out to sea. No one has ever seen them again. This chalice belonged to one of the churches. It is truly incredible that Água knew that it was buried there!"

Patting Água on the head as he sat there in the shade contentedly, Natalia said, "Father, I am beginning to think that we have only just begun to see the amazing things that Água can do." And with that they continued on their way.

Chapter 23

Arriving within a few minutes at the open market, Father Peres quickly helped Natalia locate a stall where fruits and vegetables were sold. He introduced her to the owner, Senhora Batista.

"Senhora, I would like you to meet Natalia and her dog, Água, who have travelled here from Salema to purchase fruit for her sick mother. They stayed at the church last night and will head back as soon as they fill these fishing nets with your delicious fruit."

"Ah, you have brought the young lady to the right place, *Padre*. I sell the freshest fruit in all of the Algarve! Natalia, your mama, does she have *escorbuto*?"

Natalia nodded silently.

"Well, then, she will surely be well again soon with this fine fruit and all of God's healing powers! And I will send you to my dear friend down the way to purchase some healing herbs that will help to make her strong again."

Senhora Batista carefully selected the best oranges and put them in the four small nets. Natalia would carry two. The other two she tied together and hung over Água's back, one net on each side. This way they were able to carry much more fruit back to Salema, enough to last until another trip could be made to Lagos.

Senhora Batista insisted on giving Natalia extra fruit and some cheese at no cost so that she and Água would have something to eat on the way home. And she fed him a few sardines, too. "You are most kind, Senhora. *Muito obrigada.*" (Thank you very much.)

Senhora Batista gave Natalia a big hug and kissed her on both cheeks.

"Take care, my child," she said. She directed Father Peres to a stall just down the street, so he and Natalia and Água were on their way once more.

Chapter 24

Their visit with Senhora Batista's friend, Senhora Veloso, went quickly. Once again, Father Peres introduced Natalia and Água and explained their mission. The Senhora sold only herbs, and she advised Natalia on the best ones to purchase to help make her mother strong again. She, too, wished Natalia well. Father Peres then walked with Natalia and Água back to the outskirts of the city where the path back to Salema started.

"God bless you and your family, Natalia. I will pray for your mother's recovery. She is truly blessed to have such a wonderful daughter." He then turned to Água. "And bless you, too, brave fellow. I feel that you have travelled far in your life and that you have far to go. God be with you."

And with that, Natalia and Água went on their way, each carrying their precious cargo. Father Peres watched them until they were out of sight and then turned back toward town, back to his work at the *Igreja de Santo Antonio*.

Chapter 25

Água seemed to feel Natalia's sense of urgency as they walked along, and he did not go off the trail or chase any birds. Every now and then, they saw a colorful Woodchat Shrike or a Sardinian Warbler fly past, but Água merely glanced at them and kept walking.

Soon it was time to stop for a rest and to eat lunch. Again, they stopped in the shade – this time under an ancient, twisted cork tree. Natalia took the bulging nets off of Água's back and then set down her own. They both stretched and then lay down for a few minutes.

As they rested, Natalia stroked Água's back and talked softly to him. "Água, I never would have been able to make this journey on my own. It is truly a miracle that you appeared when you did. How can I ever thank you? I feel so terrible about giving you to Dom Filipe, but I must keep my word. Oh, Água, can you ever forgive me?"

In answer, Água moved closer to Natalia and laid his head on her leg, giving her silent reassurance that all would be well. She sat up and hugged him close and then took out the food that Senhora Batista had given them. They ate quickly, and then Natalia picked a small bouquet for Mama. They loaded up again and set off, their steps now quick and light. They would soon be back home!

Chapter 26

The women of Salema noticed Natalia and Água as soon as they crested the small rise just outside the village. Great cries of joy went up, and they rushed to help them with the treasured fruit. They all immediately headed to the little hut where Olivia lay quietly, still weak and very ill. Natalia and Água hurried in.

"Mama! Mama! We are back! And we have the fresh fruit and herbs that you need to make you strong again! I will cut some for you to eat right away."

A proud light shone in Mama's eyes as she looked at Natalia. "I knew that you would be strong and brave, my daughter. I had no doubt." Then she looked at Água, who had sat down right next to her. She shakily reached out her hand and patted his head. "And you, dear Água. Never has anyone had a more loyal friend and companion than you have been to my Natalia."

Água gently laid his head on the bed at her side, keeping watch while Natalia joined the neighbors in the other room to unpack the fruit and cut some for her Mama. Mama drifted off to sleep again, a soft, peaceful smile on her lips, a vigilant Água at her side.

Chapter 27

More than a week had passed since the trip to Lagos. Natalia could see improvement in her Mama every day. She was now able to sit up in bed on her own, and the color in her face was slowly returning.

The men were still having great fortune fishing every day, but they were not out today. It was Sunday, a day of rest and for taking time to give thanks to the Lord for his goodness. Great happiness was in the air of the little village, and today was to be a day of celebration. But even though Natalia was happy, too, her heart was heavy. She knew that soon Dom Filipe would be coming to collect Água as payment for his loan.

During the week, Água had stayed close by Natalia's side. When he was not out on the boat, he followed her everywhere. No distance was too small for him to follow her, even as she moved around the little hut. They were inseparable. Then, the day Natalia was dreading arrived. On Sunday, Dom Filipe knocked on the door.

Chapter 28

Natalia knew he was there before he even knocked. Água had suddenly stiffened and growled low in his throat, just as he had done the last time Dom Filipe had visited. She touched Água's head to quiet him and went to the door, Água at her heels. There stood Dom Filipe, an insincere smile on his face, his eyes hard. He looked down at Água and said, "Natalia, *my dear*, may I come in? I would like to pay my respects to your mother and check on her progress, which I hear has been remarkable!"

Though she did not want to, Natalia politely invited him in. She stepped into the other room and told Mama that Dom Filipe wished to have a word with her. Mama nodded and answered, "Yes. I would like to have a word with him as well. Natalia, please wait outside with Água."

Though she did not want to leave Mama alone with Dom Filipe, Natalia could tell by the stubborn look on her mother's face that she was determined to meet with him. "Very well, Mama. We shall be right outside the door."

Natalia brought Dom Filipe to her mother and then stepped outside with Água. He, too, was not comfortable leaving Mama alone. He stood at attention right next to the door, listening intently for any sign of trouble.

"Dom Filipe, how kind of you to visit," Mama said when Natalia and Água had gone outside. "I must thank you for your kindness to my family in lending us the money to purchase the fruit and herbs I needed to get well. You are so generous."

"Ah, Senhora, you are most welcome! I could do nothing else. I heard of your family's distress and knew that I could be of assistance, so naturally I did all that I could. Is there any other way I may be of service to you and your family?"

"Well, Dom Filipe," Mama said, "my husband tells me that you made a bargain with my daughter: the money we needed for the fruit in exchange for the dog, Água. Is this true?"

"Yes, Senhora, it is true. My fleet will benefit greatly by having such a magnificent animal to help out. My crews travel far, much farther than local fishermen. A dog like this one will greatly increase their haul of fish, and I will become even more wealthy and powerful!"

"Please, Dom Filipe, I know that this is a lot to ask, but I beg of you to give us the chance to repay you for the fruit in some other way. The men are bringing in large amounts of fish every day now, and soon we will be able to pay you back the money we borrowed. Água and my daughter ... they have a special bond. Please, Dom Filipe, do not take him away from her. I beg of you!"

"Senhora, I do not wish to distress you, but I am afraid I cannot agree to your request. The dog is mine, and I shall be taking him with me now! Goodbye!" And with that, Dom Filipe turned on his heel and headed back to the door, flinging it open wide and stalking outside.

Chapter 29

Natalia and Água quickly stepped aside as Dom Filipe stormed out the door. She looked up to see her mother slowly walking toward them, the first time she had been out of bed in two months! Her joy at seeing her mother walking quickly gave way to dismay as she watched Dom Filipe take a rope with a slip knot on the end and try to put it around Água's neck like a leash. Água growled a warning and moved backward.

Just then Natalia noticed that they were no longer alone. All of their friends from the village had heard that Dom Filipe had come back for Água, and a small crowd had gathered in front of the hut. Papa and Tomas worked their way through the crowd to join Natalia.

Everyone watching the scene gasped in horror as Dom Filipe suddenly lunged at Água, trying to grab him by the scruff of the neck and hold him so that he could catch him in the slip knot. Again, Água easily dodged him and quickly leapt into the crowd and then ran toward the water.

In all the excitement, no one had noticed that the mist of *Névoa do milagre* had once again silently crept in along the coast … but Água had. He dashed down the sandy beach toward the pier that was suddenly shrouded in fog. Dom Filipe ran after him, calling angrily, but Água did not slow down. Everyone ran as fast as they could after them to see what would happen. Mama stayed standing in the doorway, her hands clutched in prayer in front of her.

Água stopped on the beach just before the dock. He looked back at Natalia. Once again, his right eye closed as he winked at her. Then with a sharp bark, he turned and ran down the pier. Natalia was not sure if her eyes were playing tricks on her or not, but she thought she caught a glimpse of another dog outlined in the fog. As Água disappeared into the swirling mist, Natalia expected to hear a loud SPLASH! as he jumped in the water, just as she had heard many times before. And she prayed that he would swim as far and as fast as he could to get away from Dom Filipe.

But the splash never came.

And slowly, the *Névoa do milagre* disappeared under the warm, Portuguese sun. Água disappeared as quietly as he had come, leaving behind a little village that would never be the same again and a legend about the miraculous dog that had come from the sea.

Epilogue

Six months after Água had left, Natalia was getting ready for bed. As always, she said her prayers and then went to the window to close the curtains. As she did so, the full moon revealed a soft, wispy fog rolling in off the sea. Joyous, she ran to the door of the hut and threw it open, expecting to see Água once more. But she saw nothing.

"Água!" she called. " Água, come here, boy!" In response she heard a tiny whimper, not a sound that she had ever heard Água make. It came from off to her right. She moved toward the sound. There, huddled up against the corner of the hut, she found a small black bundle of wet, curly fur. A Portuguese Water Dog puppy! Natalia gently reached for him and held him close to her as she stepped back into the hut.

As she had done with Água, she found a rag to dry him. Then she held him up and looked at him closely. His coloring was different from Água's. The puppy was mostly black with a curly coat. He had a white blaze on his chest and big white paws. He had just a dot of white on the end of his tail, a flag just as Água's had been.

"What is your name, boy?" Natalia asked softly. The puppy gave a little yip. "Oh, I see, you are not a boy! You are a girl! Well, in that case, I shall call you *Luar* (Moonlight), for you came to me on the night of a full moon."

And so she did.

~ The End

Coming Soon:
Água's next adventure!

Join Água as he continues his time travelling adventures, appearing in Washington, D.C., during the War of 1812. As the British invade the capital in 1814, he befriends First Lady Dolley Madison, helping her escape the burning White House and saving precious pieces of American history.

Timeline of Portugal and the Algarve
(and the arrival of the Portuguese Water Dog)

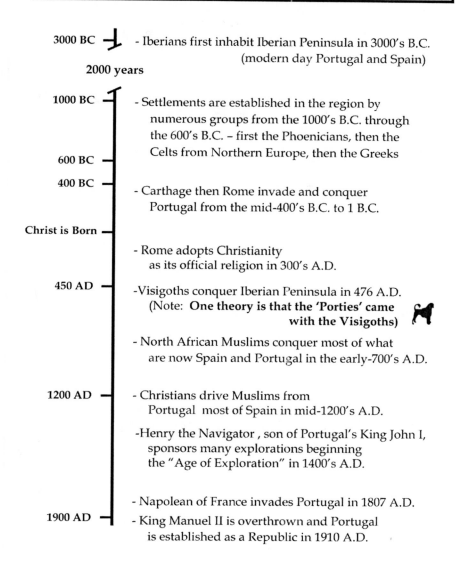

3000 BC — Iberians first inhabit Iberian Peninsula in 3000's B.C.
(modern day Portugal and Spain)

2000 years

1000 BC — Settlements are established in the region by
numerous groups from the 1000's B.C. through
the 600's B.C. – first the Phoenicians, then the
600 BC — Celts from Northern Europe, then the Greeks

400 BC — Carthage then Rome invade and conquer
Portugal from the mid-400's B.C. to 1 B.C.

Christ is Born —

- Rome adopts Christianity
as its official religion in 300's A.D.

450 AD — Visigoths conquer Iberian Peninsula in 476 A.D.
(Note: **One theory is that the 'Porties' came
with the Visigoths**)

- North African Muslims conquer most of what
are now Spain and Portugal in the early-700's A.D.

1200 AD — Christians drive Muslims from
Portugal most of Spain in mid-1200's A.D.

- Henry the Navigator , son of Portugal's King John I,
sponsors many explorations beginning
the "Age of Exploration" in 1400's A.D.

- Napolean of France invades Portugal in 1807 A.D.
1900 AD — King Manuel II is overthrown and Portugal
is established as a Republic in 1910 A.D.

Sources:

Braund, Kathryn. *The New Complete Portuguese Water Dog.* Second Edition. New York: Wiley Publishing, 1997. Print.

CIA – The World Fact Book https://www.cia.gov/library/publications/the-world-factbook/

Nation Master http://www.nationmaster.com/index.php

Portuguese Water Dog Club of America, Inc. www.pwdca.org

World Book Online, Loudoun County Public Library, Leesburg, Virginia

"Portugal." *The World Book Encyclopedia of People and Places.* 2003. Print.

Steves, Rick. *Rick Steves' Portugal.* Berkeley: Avalon Travel, 2009. Print.

Yahoo! Babel Fish http://babelfish.yahoo.com/

LaVergne, TN USA
14 November 2009
164103LV00005B/1/P